The Loneliest Kitten

Holly Webb

Illustrated by Sophy Williams

For everyone at Birch Copse Primary School

www.hollywebbanimalstories.com

STRIPES PUBLISHING LIMITED
An imprint of the Little Tiger Group
1 Coda Studios, 189 Munster Road,
London SW6 6AW

A paperback original
First published in Great Britain in 2019

Text copyright © Holly Webb, 2019
Illustrations copyright © Sophy Williams, 2019
Author photograph copyright © Nigel Bird

ISBN: 978-1-78895-039-8

A CIP catalogue record for this book is available
from the British Library.

Printed and bound in the UK.

10 9 8 7 6 5 4 3 2 1

Chapter One

"Take off your trainers!" Mum yelped as Darcy and Will reached the back door.

"Sorry, Mum." Darcy kicked off her trainers and held on to Will's arm so he could do the same. Even though it was the beginning of the summer holidays, the weather wasn't very summery. "The garden's really wet and it's all muddy in front of the football goal…"

"I can see that. Will looks like he's been rolling in it."

"I was the goalkeeper!" Will said enthusiastically.

Dad came into the kitchen and stared at Darcy and Will. "Wow. What happened to you two?"

"We were playing football." Darcy frowned. "You're home early."

"That's why I called you in," said

Mum. She had an 'I've got a secret' face on, Darcy thought. "You'd better go and get changed. And Will, I think you probably need a shower. We're going on a trip, somewhere really exciting, but it's a surprise."

"I'm here so I can come too," Dad added. "I wish I'd been here earlier, then I could have joined in your football game. I'm nearly as good a goalie as Will!"

"Nobody is better than me," Will said smugly. "I saved almost all of Darcy's shots."

Darcy made a face over the top of Will's head to say that he hadn't really and Mum smiled. Will was actually very good for someone who was only six. He was tall too – not that much shorter than Darcy, and she was three years older.

"Go and get changed, Darcy," said Mum. "And don't worry, there's no need to dress up. Shorts and a T-shirt are fine."

"Come on, Will, I'll turn the shower on for you," Dad suggested.

Darcy could hear Will trying to quiz Dad as they went upstairs. "Where are we going? Will there be pizza? Can I wear my Batman outfit?" She was curious too. They did sometimes go on surprise days out in the summer holidays – the best one had been to the seaside, with fish and chips on the beach – but that was usually for the whole day, not in the middle of the afternoon.

She hurried into her bedroom and

changed out of her muddy tracksuit bottoms and football shirt. Luckily Mum had put her hair in Dutch plaits that morning and it still looked OK, even after playing football. She just had to scrub away the mud from under her fingernails.

Will was back downstairs soon after, looking very clean and a bit damp.

"Where are we going?" he kept asking as Mum and Dad hurried them out to the car.

"*Shh*," Darcy whispered. "It's a surprise. Surprises are good. Don't spoil it."

"I want to *know*," her little brother muttered crossly. "I don't like surprises."

"Five minutes," Dad promised from the driver's seat.

Darcy and Will peered eagerly out of the car windows, trying to think where they might be going – Darcy thought they were quite close to where her friend Emma lived. Then a few minutes later Dad pulled up outside a long low building.

Darcy read the sign outside: Haven Animal Rescue. She unclipped her seat belt and reached over to grab Dad's shoulder. "Are we … do you mean … are we really—" She swallowed hard and started again.

"Are we going to get a cat?"

"A cat!" Will squeaked.

Darcy had been trying to persuade her parents to get a pet for ages. She hadn't been sure whether they should get a cat or a dog.

Emma had a dog and she kept telling Darcy about all the naughty things he had done. Buster had eaten two of Emma's lunch boxes (not what was inside them, the actual box!) and her favourite flip-flops. Emma still loved him loads, but he was a menace.

Darcy and Will's gran loved cats and she had two beautiful ones. When they went to see Gran, if Darcy was very lucky, Pippin or Smudge might get on her knee. Darcy loved it when they sat there and let her stroke them. It would be amazing to have a cat to make a fuss of all the time. A cat of their own might even decide to sleep on Darcy's bed.

Mum loved cats too, but Dad wasn't so keen – he said they would need a lot of looking after.

"I thought you'd said no!" Darcy wrapped her arms round Dad's neck and hugged him. "Well, I realized it's Mum who's at home most of the time," Dad pointed out. "She'll end up looking after it, so she should be the one to make the decision."

Dad was right, Darcy thought. Her mum worked from home in a little office under their stairs.

"But we'll help," she said eagerly.

"We can feed the cat. And I can vacuum up the fur." Cat hair all over the carpets had been one of the things Dad was concerned about. "I like vacuuming," she assured him.

"Can we go and see the cat *now*?" Will begged and Dad laughed and opened the car door.

"Come on then!"

"We made an appointment to see a litter of kittens," Mum explained as they went into the building. "There are four of them, and they're old enough to be rehomed now. When you went round to Gran's the other day, a lady from the shelter came to check the house to make sure we weren't too close to any busy roads or anything like that. They rang me yesterday to say we can definitely have a kitten! But –" she gave Darcy and Will a serious look – "they only rehome pets to people who have older children, because you need to be sensible to be around a cat or a dog. So you must show them how sensible you can be. No arguing!"

Will's eyes widened and he nodded seriously.

"We'll be good," Darcy promised. She and Will had got into a fight at Gran's house once, because Will wouldn't stop tickling her. She'd been really cross and yelled at him, and Pippin had run away and hidden under Gran's bed. It was ages until she would come out and Darcy had felt so guilty. She couldn't help arguing with Will sometimes, but she definitely didn't want to upset a kitten.

"Hi, I'm Lucy Adams." Mum smiled at the woman behind the reception desk. "We're here to see some kittens."

"That's right, we're expecting you. Wait here for a minute and Jesse will come and collect you – he's one of our staff. We have a meeting room where you can get to know the kittens before you choose."

Choose! Darcy looked around the reception area at the photos of cats and dogs on the walls. They were beautiful and all of them were staring hopefully out of the picture, as if begging to be taken home.

How were they going to choose which kitten should be theirs?

A young man in a green fleece with the Haven logo came in and grinned at Darcy and Will. "Hi – you're here to meet the kittens?"

"That's right." Mum squeezed Darcy's hand. "We're really excited."

"Great. They're in our meeting room down here." Jesse led them along a corridor lined with more gorgeous photos and opened a door. "It's OK, they're shut in," he explained as Dad peered in, looking a bit worried. "They aren't going to make a run for it."

"Oh, look…" Mum said softly as she went in. "Aren't they sweet, Darcy?"

But Darcy didn't say anything. She was too busy watching. Jesse was unlatching a wire crate and three tiny kittens were starting to nose curiously at the door. They climbed and wriggled and stomped all over each other, trying to get out and see what was going on.

"Look at the ginger one!" Will gasped as a ginger kitten launched itself over the top of two tabbies, bouncing on to the floor. It sniffed nosily at Dad's trainers and then batted one paw at the dangling laces.

The tabby kittens stumbled out behind the ginger one and gazed thoughtfully up at Mum and Darcy.

"Do they know we want to take one of them home?" Darcy whispered to her mum.

"You're actually the first family these kittens have met," Jesse said, "so they probably don't know what's going on. We've had them for a few weeks, with their mum. We're planning to rehome her with one of the kittens, and the others either on their own or together."

"Just one for us!" Dad said anxiously. "We're not very experienced pet owners. We only want one kitten."

Darcy closed her mouth firmly. She'd been just about to say that maybe they should have two kittens, but she didn't want to put Dad off.

"Aren't there four of them?" she
asked Jesse, looking around the room.
There were definitely only three
kittens out. The two tabbies were still
by the crate, watching cautiously, and
the ginger one was now trying to climb
up Dad's jeans.

Jesse nodded. "Look…" he
murmured, and Darcy crouched down
to look inside the wire crate. It was
padded with a rumpled
fleece blanket and
peering out from
under the folds
was a small,
worried-looking
tabby and
white face.

Chapter Two

The kitten had the pinkest nose that
Darcy had ever seen on a cat. It was
such a bright pink that it almost
looked like it would glow in the dark.
The kitten stared back at Darcy with
round, yellow-green eyes and then
it stepped out from under the folds
of the blanket. Now Darcy could see
that it looked different to the other

two tabbies. They were tabby all over, with grey-brown paws. This kitten was tabby with a neat white shirt front and sparklingly white paws. It had a very cute white chin too, as if it was white with a tabby mask over its eyes and ears.

"Oh, that's a very sweet kitten," Mum said and Jesse laughed.

"I know – I love his markings."

The tabby and white kitten edged slowly out of the crate and then sat down in front of it. He still looked nervous – perhaps he was scared of the room full of people, Darcy thought. Will was so desperate to make Jesse think he was sensible that he hadn't said a word, but even though they were being quiet, they were still very big compared to a kitten.

The kitten lifted one of his front paws, licked at it and passed it vaguely in the direction of his ears. Darcy had a feeling he wasn't really trying to wash, it was just giving him something to do, so he could pretend he hadn't noticed all these people staring at him.

Now that he was washing, Darcy noticed the underside of his paws – the pads were the same neon-pink as his nose. They stood out brightly against the white fur, like little pink beans.

"He's gorgeous," she said, looking hopefully at Mum to see if she felt the same way. Maybe she'd fallen in love with one of the others?

But Mum was looking at the kitten washing too, with the same sort of face that Darcy imagined she was making. "Isn't he?" she agreed.

"He's washing his *ears*," Will said in a tiny whisper. "He's so clever!"

Dad sighed. "I take it we're having this one then?"

"Don't you like him?" Darcy asked indignantly.

"Um... He's definitely cute," Dad admitted. "I'm just not a big cat person."

"Sorry," Darcy said to Jesse, hoping this didn't put him off them.

"It's OK." Jesse grinned. "I'm pretty sure this one will win your dad over."

They walked back to the car with the kitten in a cat carrier – it had been in the boot of the car the whole time, but Darcy and Will hadn't known. Mum told them she had been to the pet shop and bought it the same day the shelter had done the home check. She'd bought a cat basket, some food bowls and kitten food too. They were all hidden in the shed in the garden.

"I haven't got any toys or a collar yet, though. I thought you two would like to help choose those," she said.

"What will the kitten play with when we get home?" Will asked, frowning.

"Kittens play with everything." Mum laughed. "You saw that ginger one trying to eat Dad's shoelaces. They like bits of string, balls of paper. Sunbeams even. Don't worry, I expect our kitten will be too busy exploring to miss having any toys."

Our kitten. Darcy smiled – it sounded so good. She watched as Mum settled the cat carrier on the back seat between her and Will. Darcy could just see the kitten through the spaces in the sides. He was huddled up in a little ball at the end and he didn't look very happy.

"It's OK," Darcy whispered as Mum started the car. "I expect you don't like being shut up in there. But we'll be home soon and then you can get out."

From inside the carrier, the kitten heard her whispering, but he didn't know what she meant. He didn't like this. The carrier had been swinging about and now it was moving strangely, so that his insides felt like they were being left behind. The car lurched

to a stop and the carrier juddered. The kitten slid forwards with a little mew of fright.

The carrier had a soft blanket on the bottom, folded up like a cushion. He remembered a blanket like that from the crate back at the shelter. It was soft and warm, and inside it would be dark. He'd feel safe in there, he decided. He patted at the edge of the blanket with his claws, ruffling it up into a fold so he could sneak underneath. It made a cosy little cave and he crept inside.

"I don't think he liked being in the car," Darcy said, looking worriedly at the small hump of blanket that was the kitten. "He mewed when we had to stop at the lights and then he hid in the blanket." They had put the carrier down in the corner of the kitchen but the kitten didn't seem to want to come out.

"Poor little thing," Mum said, crouching down to look at the rumpled blanket. "I did try to drive as slowly as I could. But I suppose he's never been in a car before. He'll be OK soon. Right now, though, I think we need to be patient and just leave him alone."

Darcy nodded. She knew Mum was right, even though she was desperate to play with the kitten. Jesse had told them that the kittens had been born at the shelter after their mum had been found abandoned. They'd never been anywhere else. Their kitten must feel like everything was different and scary.

No wonder he wanted to stay wrapped up in a blanket.

"Maybe he'll come out if we put down food for him?" Will suggested hopefully.

"He's in a blanket!" Darcy pointed out. "He won't see the food."

"But he might be able to smell it," Mum said thoughtfully. "It's worth a try. We want him to like being here, so feeding him would be a good start."

She fetched the bag of kitten food and shook some of the little biscuits into the kitten's new bowl. It rattled as the biscuits fell in and Darcy saw the blanket twitch.

The kitten was thinking. He knew that noise and he was hungry. But outside the warm, safe cocoon of blanket there were different smells and the oddness of being away from his mother and the other kittens. Did he want to come out?

He was *very* hungry, though. He could smell the food now – the scent was creeping across the kitchen and it was making him feel even hungrier. His nose poked out from under the fold of blanket and he eyed the open door of the carrier. He could see the bowl right there, with the girl and boy sitting on the floor behind it.

When they saw him watching, the girl patted the boy's arm and they edged backwards, leaving a bit more space between them and the bowl. That was better. It wasn't quite as scary if they weren't so close.

The kitten stumbled out over the folds of blanket and stood hesitantly in the doorway of the carrier. Then he crept over to the bowl and started to eat, keeping one eye on the children. It seemed ages since he'd last been fed and there was a good bowlful here. He had to go more slowly towards the end and he even left a few biscuits. He then sat down heavily and ran his paw over his whiskers.

He could see the children looking at him. They seemed a lot less frightening now that they'd been sitting still for so long and he was feeling much better after the food, although he was a bit sleepy. Thoughtfully, he padded towards them and sniffed at the girl's hands. She was less scary than the boy since she kept so very still. The smaller boy wriggled. The girl didn't move, even when the kitten licked at her fingers – she shivered a little, that was all.

The kitten sat down. He was very full and he was getting sleepy, and the girl's foot was in just the right place for his chin to lean on. He slumped against her and then, seconds later, he let out a tiny kitten snore.

Chapter Three

"Oh, Charlie! Where's your collar gone?"

"Not another one!" Mum turned round and Darcy held up the kitten to show her. Charlie nuzzled happily against her fingers.

"Look – no collar."

"I don't know how he does it." Mum stared at Charlie and shook her head.

"Monster," she said lovingly. "It's lucky I bought you a spare last time, isn't it? Hold on to him a minute, Darcy, I'll get the new one."

The kitten had settled in well after his shy start. He was funny and clever and Mum was right that he would play with anything. He adored Dad too. He seemed to know that Dad wasn't as much of a cat fan so he had to be the perfect pet. Whenever Dad sat on the sofa, Charlie would appear as if by magic. Then he'd try to climb up the side of his jeans so he could collapse exhausted on Dad's lap. Dad pretended it was nothing, but Darcy could tell he loved it. He'd stroke Charlie over and over, running one finger all the way down from the top of his head to his tail.

They had argued for ages over what to call him. Will thought he ought to be called Mario, like the Nintendo character, but Darcy didn't think he looked like a Mario. He needed something that was cuddly but showed his cheeky side too. Like the way he could get on to the kitchen table in less than ten seconds and drink the milk out of her cereal bowl before she was back from the fridge with a glass of juice.

It was actually Dad who came up

with the name. He said the kitten reminded him of someone he'd been at school with – his friend Charlie was always getting into trouble, but then he'd look really innocent and sorry and everyone forgave him. Dad suggested it just after the kitten had been sick on his shoe.

Charlie's worst trick was getting rid of his collar. "How did you do it this time?" Darcy murmured, tickling him under the chin. "I'll look for it in the garden later, Mum."

Ever since Charlie had been old enough to go outside, Darcy and Will had been finding collars in the flower beds and Hannah, who lived next door, had come round with one that had been in her lavender bush. Charlie seemed to have a gift for hooking his collar on things. The collars had special catches that came open if the cat was trapped or caught on something and Charlie had figured out exactly how to get rid of them.

He wriggled as Mum clipped on another collar and Darcy was sure he glared at her. He was probably working out how to get himself out of this one.

"Have you got your bag packed ready for tomorrow, Darcy?"

"No." Darcy sighed. She was looking forward to going back to school and seeing everyone, but after seven weeks of holidays it was going to be hard getting up early every morning. And it was going to be even harder leaving Charlie behind after spending all those weeks playing with him. "Charlie's going to miss us, Mum. You must promise you'll make a fuss of him, even when you're working."

Mum laughed. "Yes, of course I will. I don't think I'll have a choice anyway. He'll be up on my desk stomping about on my keyboard, I bet."

"I suppose…" Darcy agreed. "I'll go and sort out my stuff now, and I'll take Charlie with me."

Darcy carried the kitten up to her room and put him on her bed. She watched, smiling, as Charlie stomped up and down the duvet, his paws sinking in with every step. Then he peered thoughtfully over the edge of her bed and scrambled down the side to explore the bedroom.

Darcy got her school backpack out
of the wardrobe. Mum had bought
her new pencils and things a couple
of weeks before but she had forgotten
where she'd put them – her room was
a bit of a mess. Charlie stalked a ball
of paper across the carpet and went
wriggling under the bed for a while.
He came out with his white bits all
covered in fluffy dust and Darcy had
to brush him off.

"You're so funny," she whispered as she blew dust off his whiskers and he sneezed and nearly fell over. "I'm going to miss you but I promise I'll come home straight after school. We'll spend ages playing with you then. And Emma's going to come round too. You like her, don't you?"

Charlie climbed on to Darcy's lap and curled up there, batting sleepily at the ends of her hair. Darcy sighed. Even though Mum had promised to try, Charlie was going to be so bored without her and Will to play with.

"Mum! Mum! Guess what!" Darcy came flying out of school that first afternoon with Emma dashing behind her. She flung herself gleefully at her mum.

"I can't guess," Mum said, staggering backwards. "What's happened?"

"Mrs Jennings is organizing a girls' football team – and me and Emma are going to be in it! It's in a schools' league and everything! There'll be practice on Tuesdays and Thursdays, and matches too. That's OK, isn't it? I can do it, can't I? There's a form you have to sign. Mrs Jennings even showed us the kit – it's green – it's so cool, Mum!"

"Wow! Yes… That should be fine, I think. Luckily it doesn't clash with swimming on a Wednesday. You're going to be busy!"

"I can do it, though, can't I, Mum?" Emma asked her mum hopefully, and she nodded.

"Of course. Well done, you two!"

"It's going to be amazing!" Darcy hugged Emma and they danced around until Will came across the playground, looking a bit tired and grumpy.

"We're going to be in the football team!" Darcy told him excitedly.

"Oh – great. Can we go home and see Charlie now?"

Darcy blinked. Just for those few minutes since Mrs Jennings had come to their classroom at the end of school, she'd completely forgotten about Charlie – on the very first day they'd left him alone. She suddenly felt guilty.

"Was he OK today, Mum?" she asked anxiously.

"I think so. He played with the cat dancer toy and then he slept on my knee while I was working. Still, he'll be pleased to see you two."

Darcy nodded. "We'll play with him for ages when we get home."

"Don't forget your football practice," Emma reminded her. "Mrs Jennings said we need to practise at home too."

Charlie hopped down the stairs a step at a time as he heard them coming up the path. He'd spent most of the day asleep, with spells of wandering around the house looking for Darcy and Will. Their mum was in her little office under the stairs, but she just kept typing around him, even when he tried to catch her fingers to nibble. It wasn't much fun.

As the front door opened he galloped across the hallway and twined lovingly in and out of Darcy's and Will's legs. They crouched down and fussed over him and Darcy stroked his ears just the way he liked it. Charlie purred and purred – he'd missed them so much.

He followed the children eagerly as they went into the kitchen and accepted a little bit of Darcy's cheese sandwich. Where had they been all day? They'd never gone away for so long before. Charlie bounced around excitedly as Darcy waved the cat dancer toy. It was his favourite – he loved stalking it up the hallway, but every time he pounced, Darcy would whisk it up out of the way, so that his paws just grazed the dancing feathers. He had more of a chance when he played with Will, as sometimes Will wasn't quick enough and Charlie managed to get a mouthful of feathers.

But after they'd played for a little while, Darcy disappeared upstairs and came down in different clothes. She was going into the garden, Charlie realized, and he hurried out of the door after her. He loved being outside. There were so many good hiding places and interesting smells in the garden. Sometimes there were bees too, and butterflies. Charlie was desperate to catch a fat furry bumblebee. They blundered about just in front of his nose but somehow he'd never managed to nab one.

Whatever Darcy was doing was

probably even more interesting than a bee, though. He followed her down the lawn and sprang delightedly on the football when she tapped it with her foot and it rolled across the grass. She laughed and tapped it again and he raced after the ball, flinging himself on top of it and then rolling off on to the grass. He sprang up and lunged again as Darcy shimmied the ball across the grass, and this time as the ball rolled he went with it, nosediving to the ground.

Darcy crouched down next to him. She looked at him worriedly as he shook his whiskers. "Sorry, Charlie. Did it squish you? Are you OK? Maybe I'd better take you inside, kitten. I don't want you to get hurt."

She scooped him up and slipped him back inside the kitchen door, and then she flipped the switch on the cat flap so he couldn't follow her back out again.

Charlie glared indignantly at the cat flap. Darcy had been away all day and now he wasn't allowed out to play with her! He stalked across the kitchen and sat down grumpily in his basket. Why had Darcy stopped him playing? He'd only wanted to be with her. What had he done wrong?

Chapter Four

Charlie could see the children were
going to disappear the next day too –
they had bags and coats and everything
was a rush. When he tried to get on
the table to drink the milk out of
Will's cereal bowl, Mum scooped him
back down with a firm, "No!" and then
she added, "Oh no, he's lost his collar
again! I'll have to get him another one."

Darcy made a fuss of him when she gave him his breakfast but she was dashing about and didn't want to play. Charlie went to sit a little way up the stairs and watched as the children pulled on their shoes. Why were they going off again?

When Will ran back into the kitchen
to fetch his forgotten lunch box, Charlie
padded softly down the stairs and
sniffed at his backpack, trying to work
out what was happening. The zip was
open and the bag smelled strange –
musty, like leftover packed lunches. It
was interesting… Charlie put one paw
in, and then the other, and sniffed at the
grubby crumbs at the bottom of the bag.
Then he sneezed.

"Look at Charlie! He's in my bag!"

Charlie looked up to see Will
crouching over him, laughing.

"I think he wants to come to school!"

"Poor Charlie – he's missing you,"
Mum said. "You'd better get him out,
Will. We need to go."

Charlie wriggled as Will gently

reached under his front legs and lifted him out of the bag. Taking him out only made him think that the bag was exciting…

He watched gloomily as the front door slammed behind them, and then stalked back into the kitchen to his basket.

Perhaps they'd play with him when they got home?

Darcy and Will did their best to fit in looking after Charlie with all their school stuff. But Darcy was really excited about being in the football team. She'd always loved kicking a ball about but now she was seriously trying to practise her football skills. And it wasn't just practising – she got Dad to take her to the library to find football books too. If she wasn't outside playing football, she was curled up on the sofa reading about it.

A couple of weeks after term had started, Charlie padded into the living room to see if Darcy would play with him. She and Will had just got back from school and he was so pleased to see them. He snuggled up between Darcy and the cushions for a while, but he'd been dozing for most of the day and he wanted to dash about and chase things, not help her read. He tried patting at the pages and even sitting on the book, but she just kept moving him. In the end he jumped down from the sofa and went to see what Will was doing.

Charlie could hear him growling as he came into the kitchen. Will was glaring at a worksheet on the table – then he started to rub out what he'd just written and ended up throwing the rubber halfway across the table so it bounced on to the floor.

A game! At last!

Charlie sprang at it, batting the rubber with his paw and enjoying the way his claws caught in it.

"Hey! I need that!" Will reached down and grabbed it back. "Sorry, Charlie. I hate homework, it's the worst thing about Year Two." He looked at Charlie again. "You've lost *another* collar! I'd better tell Mum."

Charlie sat under Will's chair,

hoping that he might throw the rubber again, but he didn't. In the end the little kitten gave up on him and popped through the cat flap out into the garden. Perhaps today would be the day he caught a bumblebee?

He padded across the grass, twitching happily as he felt the hot sun on his fur. He sat down in the middle of the lawn and washed his ears for a bit – and then all of a sudden, *there* was a bee!

It zoomed wildly across the grass in front of him, swooping down to a patch of clover. Charlie went into a hunting crouch and tried to stalk it, but the bee lumbered away before he even got close. He hurried after it, chasing it over to the lavender bush by the wall until it disappeared over into next-door's garden, buzzing happily.

Charlie stared after it, his tail twitching. He could still hear the buzzing. He'd been so close! Suddenly determined, he jumped up on to the garden bench and then made a wobbly leap on to the wooden back. He teetered there for a moment and then sprang for the wall, scrabbling hard and digging his claws into the branches of ivy. Then he was on the top of the wall, with the bee buzzing lazily across the flower beds below him.

Charlie made a rushing, scrambling climb down the other side of the wall and looked around for the bee. The fur on his back was rumpled up with the wild scramble down the wall and a little bit with fright. He hadn't expected it to be quite so high. But now, surely, he'd catch that bee?

Except it had disappeared. It had completely, utterly gone. Charlie looked around in disbelief. It wasn't fair!

A soft murmuring noise made his ears twitch – but it wasn't a bee. It was someone talking. Whoever it was had a pleasant, gentle sort of voice, a bit like Darcy when she was stroking him.

Curiously, Charlie padded down

to the fence at the end of next-door's garden and saw that there were gaps along the bottom of it – quite big gaps. He could get through there easily, no scrambling needed. He wriggled through and hesitated in the bushes, watching an old lady watering her flowerpots. She was murmuring to herself about the weather, which was warm and dry now after the wet summer.

The water drops glinted and sparkled in the sunshine and he padded a little closer. The old lady didn't see him, she just kept watering, and Charlie couldn't resist the pattering of the drops any longer. He pounced, springing at the glittering water, trying to catch the drops with his white paws.

"Oh! Where did you come from?"
the old lady gasped. "Oh dear, are you
all wet now?"

Charlie had water droplets covering
his whiskers, up his nose and in his ears.
He shook his head briskly and then
looked hopefully up at her. Was she
going to do it again? He reached up one
paw and tapped at the watering can.

"You liked it?" Laughing, the old

lady tipped up the watering can and let another shower of droplets fall down on the plants – and the kitten. Charlie batted his paws eagerly, but still he couldn't catch the water.

"I wonder where you came from?" the old lady asked thoughtfully. "I haven't seen you before, I'd remember that lovely tabby pattern." She reached down and gently stroked the top of the kitten's head. "You don't look like you're lost. You're definitely someone's pet, you're so friendly. But you don't have a collar on…"

Charlie tapped the watering can again and she sprinkled a little more water on her patio, laughing as he danced about and tried to catch the water. At last she set it down by an outside tap and walked slowly back inside. Charlie padded after her. He liked this lady. She was fussing over him just the way he wanted and the water was a lot of fun.

"Oh no, I don't think you should come inside, little one," she said gently. "You're someone else's kitten and they wouldn't want you coming in, would they? You go on back home now."

She closed the glass door and stood just inside it, watching him. Charlie stared back and then stood up, putting his front paws on the glass and peering through. He mewed sadly and saw the old lady put her hand on the sofa and try to crouch down to look at him. Then she shook her head firmly, stood up and walked away.

Charlie sat down on the patio and wailed. He wanted her to come out and play again. *No one* would play with him. He was so lonely...

Five minutes later Charlie was inside the old lady's living room, sitting on the arm of the sofa and nibbling a little cube of cheese.

Chapter Five

"Yes!" Darcy ran back to high-five Bella, who'd set up her goal. "Three-one!" She waved jubilantly at Mum and Emma, who were standing at the edge of the pitch. Emma was jumping up and down. Mrs Jennings was trying to make sure everyone got a go at playing, especially as this was their first real match, but Darcy felt a bit bad that Emma hadn't got to play for longer. She didn't seem to be upset about it, though.

Darcy had been really worried when Mrs Jennings told them about the match – after all, they'd only been a team for three weeks and they definitely needed more practice. But Mrs Jennings promised it would be really good experience, even if they lost. And now they were winning! All that skills training Darcy had been doing in the park after school had made a difference. When the final whistle went, the score was four-two and the Willow Primary team just couldn't stop talking about the match.

"Shall we go to the supermarket and get a celebration cake?" Mum suggested as Darcy got into the car. "I noticed the other day that they had some with footballs on."

"Yes, please!" Darcy leaned back in the front seat, exhausted but beaming. She loved the idea of a special celebration tea. "I can't wait for Sunday," she added happily. Mrs Jennings had arranged another match – a friendly with a local school – for that Sunday afternoon.

"Can we get Charlie some cat treats

too?" she asked as they took the cake to the tills. "I think we're out of them."

"Sure – I think they're in that aisle." Mum pointed, and Darcy hurried off.

"They were on three for two, so I got all the flavours," she explained as she came back and put them in the basket.

When they got home, Darcy went to have a shower and then came down for a piece of cake. She opened the bag of cheese-flavoured cat treats and shook them. That always made Charlie come running – he knew exactly what the noise meant!

Nothing happened and Darcy shook the bag again, this time next to the open kitchen window. She expected to see a little tabby and white blur come dashing down the garden to bang the cat flap open, but still nothing. She stood in the middle of the kitchen with the bag, looking rather lost.

"Mum, where's Charlie?"

Her mum looked up from cutting the football cake and glanced round the kitchen. "I expect he's in the garden. I should put his food down actually. I forgot we haven't fed him yet."

"So … he hasn't had any tea?" Darcy said, frowning. No tea and he wasn't coming for his favourite cat treats? That was definitely strange, and worrying…

Darcy looked all round the house for Charlie – she wondered if Mum had accidentally shut him in one of the bedrooms. But she couldn't see him anywhere. She stood in the garden and called for him, but no kitten appeared.

Mum went to look up and down the street at the front of the house. Charlie had wandered down the side path of the house before, and Darcy had found him sunbathing on the front wall. Will searched upstairs again, even going through all his toy baskets.

"I wonder where he can have got to,"

Mum said as she came back in. "He's usually good at turning up for meals, although…"

"What?" Darcy asked anxiously. "Although what, Mum?"

"Have you noticed that Charlie hasn't been around as much over the last week? And he hasn't been climbing on me while I'm working."

Darcy shook her head. "No. He's always here when we get home from school." Then she was silent for a minute. *Was* he? Would she definitely have noticed? She'd been so busy with after-school football training and all the extra practice she was doing. "Mum, do you think something's happened to him?"

"I'm sure he's fine," her mum said

encouragingly, but there was still no Charlie.

Darcy was just starting to get really panicky when the kitten appeared, popping in through the cat flap and strolling calmly across the kitchen. He looked quite surprised when Darcy swooped down and picked him up for a hug.

"We didn't know where you were!" she murmured, rubbing his ears.

Charlie blinked at her and nudged her chin with his chilly little nose. "Are you hungry?" Darcy asked him. She kept him cuddled in one arm and used the other hand to reach the bag of kitten food out of the cupboard.

Mum took over and poured biscuits into Charlie's bowl. Darcy had expected him to leap down at once and start eating but he didn't seem very interested. He just sniffed at the bag as she got it out, that was all. When she put him down next to the bowl he only nibbled a couple of mouthfuls and then he sat next to the food and started to wash. He didn't seem to be hungry at all.

"Perhaps he doesn't like it," Will suggested, looking down at the cat biscuits. "I wouldn't. It smells horrible."

"He's liked it until now," Darcy said. "Why would he suddenly change his mind?"

"Actually, I've noticed he hasn't been eating the whole bowl, recently," Mum said. "Perhaps we should cut down on how much we're giving him. If he's not growing quite as fast now he's a bit older, maybe he's not as hungry."

"Maybe..." Darcy sighed. She couldn't help feeling there was more to it. But at least it was Friday and she could keep a really careful eye on Charlie over the weekend. They didn't have much planned until her football match on Sunday afternoon so she could spend loads of time with him.

"Darcy, what *are* you doing?" Mum called out of the kitchen window.

"I'm trying to teach Charlie how to be a stunt cat," Darcy yelled back. "He high-fived me! Did you see?"

"I can see him eating a lot of cat treats," Mum said, a minute or so later.

"That's how the training works. You reward them every time they get it right. Or almost right. He's very clever," Darcy said lovingly, holding out her hand for Charlie to tap. He sniffed at her hopefully, looking for another treat.

"OK… Just don't feed him the whole bag!"

The website she'd been reading had said only to do five-minute training sessions, Darcy remembered. She didn't want Charlie to get fed up. "You're a very good boy," she told him, putting the treats in her pocket. "What shall we do now, hmm?"

She'd been trying to keep an eye on him all day but she was beginning to think that they'd been worrying about nothing. Charlie had eaten almost all his breakfast and then she'd played with him, rolling a jingly ball up and down the hallway. He'd snoozed on the arm of the sofa for a bit. Then he'd stalked a feather round her bedroom floor while she'd done her homework. Will had taken him downstairs and played with the cat dancer and then Charlie had sat under the kitchen table looking hopeful for the whole of lunch. He *might* have got the end of a cheese sandwich.

Everything was fine.

Darcy turned as she heard footsteps behind her, and saw Will coming out on to the patio.

"Play football with me?" Will asked coaxingly. "Please, Darcy? I'm bored."

"Not right now. I'm trying to play with Charlie."

"You aren't. You're just sitting there."

"Is that my football you've got?" Darcy asked suspiciously. "That's my new one!"

"It was behind that flowerpot." Will shrugged. "You should put it away if it's so special."

"You're not playing with it," Darcy said firmly. "I'm serious."

"Don't be so mean!"

"Will, that's my new ball, go and get your own!"

Will didn't answer. He smirked
at Darcy and started to kick the ball
against the garden wall.

"Mum!" Darcy yelled. "Make him
stop playing with it!"

Will looked round to see if Mum
was in the kitchen, listening, and lost
control of the ball. It went flying over
the back fence.

"Oh, now look what you've done," Darcy said furiously. "We'll never get it back."

"Sorry…" Will said shamefacedly. "I'll go round and ask for it."

"It's no good," Darcy snapped. "It didn't go next-door into Hannah's, it went behind – that's the garden for the flats. And we don't even know which flat it belongs to." Then she stopped scowling at Will and turned slowly. "Where's Charlie?"

Will looked round the garden. "I don't know."

"But I was trying to watch him. I don't believe it – this is all your fault, Will!"

Charlie wriggled underneath the fence into the old lady's garden. He adored Darcy, especially when she was playing with him or he was snuggled up next to her in a fold of duvet at night-time – but loud voices and shouting made him nervous and twitchy. He didn't like it when Darcy and Will argued. Every time they had a spat, the fur would start to prickle up along his spine and his tail lashed. The old lady's basement flat was always peaceful – there was no shouting. And she had cat treats now too.

He padded up the garden and nosed hopefully at the glass door. It was shut but one of the windows next to it was open a crack. He could definitely fit through there. He sprang up on to the

windowsill
and wriggled
his way in,
stepping
carefully
around the
photo frames
and the vase
on the inside.

There didn't seem to be
anyone at home but there was a patch
of warm sunlight on the rug so he sat
down in it and started to lick his paws.
He'd stay a while and then maybe he'd
go back and see if Darcy wanted to
play again. In a bit…

Chapter Six

"He's been gone for ages," Darcy said miserably. "Hours, Mum. He never stays away this long. It's teatime and usually he's starving. He's always sitting around looking hopeful long before we feed him."

Mum frowned. "Not for the last week or so, Darcy. Like I told you, he just doesn't seem as bothered about his food any more. That's why I cut down how much I gave him for breakfast this morning."

Darcy stared at her. She vaguely remembered Mum saying something about that the day before when Charlie hadn't turned up in time for tea, but she'd been more worried about where Charlie actually was and she hadn't really been listening. Clearly she should have been.

"And you said he hadn't been around as much," she murmured. "He wasn't bothering you while you were working… That's why I was trying to keep an eye on him today."

Her mum nodded. "I've missed him," she admitted with a worried smile. "I used to moan when he walked across the keyboard – he wasn't that helpful when I was trying to get people's accounts to balance, but actually he did make it a lot more fun…"

"And then he stopped doing it?"

"Yes… I assumed it was because he was getting a bit older and less playful. I just thought he was sleeping more." Mum nibbled her bottom lip and glanced at the cat flap as though she hoped Charlie might just pop through it.

He didn't.

"That makes sense, though," Dad said helpfully. "Cats sleep more when they're older, don't they?"

Darcy sat down on one of the kitchen chairs, her heart thumping fast. Charlie kept disappearing and he wasn't as bothered about his food. It was almost as if... She looked down at her fingers, twisting them over and over. It was almost as if he didn't think their house was home any more. He was going somewhere else. "Do you think he's got another home?" she blurted out.

"What?" Will shook his head. "He couldn't." He sounded almost angry. "Don't say that, Darcy."

"Someone else who's feeding him and playing with him…" Darcy went on unhappily. She felt really guilty. She'd been so excited about getting their own kitten, and she and Will had made such a fuss over him those first weeks. They'd loved Charlie and played with him all the time. They'd carried him about, they'd built him adventure playgrounds out of pillows and comfy beds whenever he'd looked the tiniest bit sleepy. They'd followed him anxiously once he was allowed out and started to explore the garden.

Then school had started again and Darcy had been chosen for the football team – and suddenly there were more exciting things than kittens to think about.

But she'd *had* to practise, a little voice protested inside her. It was important! Well, yes, it was – but she didn't need to have done *that* much practice, Darcy admitted to herself. And all those football books she'd borrowed from the library, because she had to be the best in the team…

Darcy winced as she remembered putting Charlie down on the floor because he would keep sitting on the exact diagram that she was trying to look at. He'd only wanted to play with her, she thought now. He hadn't understood – there had been so many weeks in the holidays when she'd wanted to do nothing *but* play. And he'd thought they would carry on as before and she'd been annoyed with him. She'd told him to stop it. Darcy felt tears pressing up behind her eyes and she sniffed.

What about Will, though? There had been Will for Charlie to play with, the little voice inside her tried to point out. Except Darcy knew quite well that Will wanted to do everything she did, because she was his big sister and he wanted to be just as grown up as she was. And because Darcy was spending all her time on football, Will was too. That's why he'd taken her ball and tried to play with it. Then while she was shouting at him about it, their kitten had given up on them and gone to find

somewhere nicer to live. Somewhere
people actually wanted him around.

The tears spilled over and Darcy
gasped out, "I don't think he wants us
any more!"

Mum and Dad had tried to convince
Darcy that she was wrong and that
Charlie loved their house, but it was
harder and harder to do that when he
still hadn't come home. And he didn't
… all night.

"He hasn't even got his collar on,"
Darcy sobbed at bedtime. "We never
remembered to go to the pet shop
and get him a new one. It's been days
since he's had a collar. If he has found

another home, the people probably think that he's a stray because they've never seen him with one."

"I wish he was better at keeping them on," Mum said, sighing.

Darcy gave a damp sort of laugh. "It isn't that he's bad at keeping them on, Mum. He takes them off on purpose. He's too clever. He rubs them against the chair legs until they come off." Her voice shook with tears again and Mum hugged her tight.

How could their clever, gorgeous, perfect kitten not want to be theirs any more?

Later that night she heard Mum and Dad talking when she went downstairs to get a drink of water. They were in the living room and they didn't know she was there. Darcy sank down on the stairs and listened, peering through the banisters.

"Do you think Darcy's right?" Dad was asking. "Someone else has adopted him?"

She heard Mum sigh. "It's possible, isn't it? We have neglected him a bit – I just hadn't realized... But to be honest, Dave, I'd rather he's being fussed over by someone than... Well, people go so quickly along this road and he's only little. Cats are terrible with roads, they can't tell how fast the cars are."

"Someone would have come and told us if he'd been hit, surely. Oh – except he hasn't got his collar on."

"Exactly," Mum said grimly. "But hopefully anyone who picked him up would have taken him to the vet and they'd scan his microchip. They'd ring us."

"Mmmm. I suppose he could be shut in somewhere… A shed, maybe, or a garage."

Darcy didn't want to listen any more. She crept slowly back upstairs to bed, but after that it took ages for her to get to sleep. She lay there, imagining Charlie trapped in a dark shed, mewing and mewing for her to come and let him out. Or frozen in the headlights of a car… That was too horrible. She buried her head in her pillow, trying not to think about it.

She still woke up early the next morning, though. They all did. Last night they'd walked up and down the road, peering over fences and walls and calling for Charlie. They'd asked all the neighbours they'd seen, but no one had spotted a kitten. They just had to keep trying, Dad said firmly. He had to be somewhere.

"We ought to find a photo of Charlie and make a poster," Mum suggested.

"Oh! Can we do it now?" Darcy asked, jumping up. She'd been trying to eat a piece of toast because Mum had said she must eat something, but it just wasn't going down.

"You hardly ate anything last night…" Mum started to say, but then she shook her head and sighed. "Actually, I'm not very hungry either. All right. Let's look through my phone for a good photo."

Darcy and Will peered over Mum's shoulder, looking at photos of Charlie. There were so many – Charlie splayed out on the sofa, legs everywhere; Charlie sitting in a cereal bowl Mum had left on the table; Charlie asleep with his nose in his food dish. Darcy felt her eyes prickling with tears again – she had to stop! It was no use crying, it wasn't going to help them find their kitten. She sniffed hard and pointed to a photo of Charlie staring out hopefully. He must have been waiting for his tea or maybe a treat. It showed off his lovely big yellow-green eyes and his tabby and white colouring.

"Yes, that's a good one," Mum agreed. "I'll download it on to my computer and we'll make it into a poster." She went to turn on the computer and Darcy followed her.

"What are we going to say?" she asked Mum. "I mean, if we think someone might have adopted Charlie, what we really want to say is 'Give us our cat back!'. But I suppose we can't…"

"We don't know for sure that is what's happened," Mum pointed out. "Though it does seem likely. What about this?" She typed quickly and then leaned back so Darcy could see.

LOST

Young tabby and white cat.
Charlie won't wear a collar
so may look like a stray but he
is a much loved family pet.
Please help us find him!

"It's perfect," Darcy agreed.

Mum added her mobile number and printed out twenty copies. "We'll start with these. If we don't hear anything, perhaps we should do some little ones to put through all the neighbours' doors."

Darcy nodded, swallowing hard. It had just hit her that they were really going to put up these posters – people were going to look at them and think, *Oh, I must keep an eye out for that poor little cat.* Of course that was a good thing, but it was horrible they had to do it. She had walked past so many posters just like this one and felt sorry about the poor lost cat and the sad owners, and now *they* were the sad owners.

"We're going to keep looking as well, though, aren't we?" she said to Mum.

"We only did our road yesterday. We ought to go round to Thirsk Way too, and the one where our gardens back on to theirs – Barrett Close, isn't it?"

"We will, don't worry," Mum said. "We can look all morning, but then we've got to take you to your football match."

Darcy stared at her. She had completely forgotten about the football match! She shook her head. "I can't! Not when Charlie's missing, Mum. I just can't. Please will you tell Mrs Jennings I can't go?"

Mum looked at her worriedly. "I'm not sure we should do that, sweetheart. You're part of a team. You'll be letting everyone else down."

"I won't – it will just mean Emma

gets more of a chance to play. Honestly, she'll be really pleased. Don't you see? I stopped looking after Charlie properly because I was so caught up with the football team. I was practising all the time and not bothering to play with him. But now I don't care if I never get to be in the team again, if only we can find Charlie and he's safe."

Mum sighed. "OK. Maybe I won't tell Mrs Jennings exactly that, but hopefully she'll understand."

Chapter Seven

Charlie had meant to go home – after
a little while. After he'd given Darcy
and Will time to calm down and stop
shouting. When they were arguing
it made the fur on the back of his
neck rise up and it hurt his ears. He'd
never bitten Darcy or Will, he'd never
wanted to, except sometimes when
they were yelling at each other and

the anger seemed to be in the air all around them. Then it made him want to nip their ankles. It was better just not to be there.

When the old lady came home with a couple of shopping bags, she'd laughed to see him curled up and snoozing on her rug. She crouched down with an effort, rubbed his ears and spoke softly to him, telling him how beautiful he was and what nice company.

"There I was feeling quite lonely and now you've come to see me," she murmured.

Charlie sat up and purred, pushing his head affectionately into her stroking hand and twining himself around her.

"It's a good thing I picked up a few more of those food sachets, isn't it? Are you hungry, little one?" She stood up and Charlie followed her eagerly into the kitchen. He *was* hungry. And after he'd eaten he was sleepy and it was so nice to curl up on the old lady's lap on the sofa. He would go back later on, under the fence and over the wall, back to Darcy and Will... But the flat was cosy and quiet and somehow, he just didn't.

Darcy listened to Mum's end of the
phone conversation with Mrs Jennings
– she sounded very apologetic. She
kept saying how much Darcy loved
football, it was just that this was
important and everyone was very
upset.

At that point, Darcy put one of the
sofa cushions over her head. It was too
weird listening to Mum describe how
miserable she was. It made her feel even
sadder. The more people who knew that
Charlie was missing, the worse it felt.
And now loads of people were going to
know, Darcy thought, sighing into the
dusty fabric of the cushion.

Dad thought putting small versions

of the poster through people's doors
was a very good idea. The neighbours
would have a copy of the flyer with
their number on if they spotted
Charlie, he pointed out, and Darcy
knew they wanted as many people as
possible to look for Charlie. But when
everyone in the street was getting a

little photo of Charlie
through their door,
it made him
seem a lot more
missing.

She and Dad
took turns to
do the houses
on their side of
the road, while
Mum and Will

did the other side. Will was enjoying it, Darcy noticed sadly. He thought it was exciting, getting to post the little notes through the letter boxes. If it had been anything else they were posting, Darcy would have liked it too. But she seemed to keep catching the photo of Charlie at just the wrong angle – he looked so sad as she squashed him through the flaps, his nose wrinkling up, his whiskers drooping. He looked like a Lost Cat.

They worked their way down the street to the side road, Thirsk Way, which led on to Barrett Close – a mirror image of their road, with its gardens joining on to theirs.

"We definitely need to deliver notes along here," Darcy said to Dad.

"Charlie was out in the garden – he could easily have gone over the back fence into one of the gardens here."

"Do you think so?" Dad said doubtfully. "Our back fence is pretty high. I'm not sure he could get over it, to be honest. I'd have thought he nipped up the side passage and out through the front garden."

Darcy shook her head. She'd seen Charlie scrambling up the side wall before and shooting up a tree as if it was a little cat ladder. He was an amazingly good climber.

"But maybe you're right," Dad said. "And it's not that far away – he could even have walked down the road and round the corner like we did. Have we got enough flyers left or do we need to go back and print some more?"

"Just about enough," Darcy said, showing him her handful. "Except there's the little block of flats that almost backs on to us. I don't know how many people live there."

"Well, let's see how far we get," Dad said, heading up the path of the nearest house.

They still had a few flyers left when they got to the flats at the end of the road, and Darcy looked at the main door uncertainly. It didn't have a letter box – should they go in and put the flyers in the pigeonholes just inside?

"Do you think we should put them under the doors of the flats?" she asked Dad. "There's no post on Sundays, is there? No one's going to come down and check those." She pointed at the pigeonholes. "We want them to look in the garden for Charlie today... I wonder which flat has the garden? Or maybe they share it?"

"Probably that one." Dad held the main door open and walked over to the door behind the staircase. "Put a note under here, Darcy."

But as Darcy crouched down to post the flyer under the door, the lock clicked and the door started to open.

A friendly voice said, "Hello! I heard you talking – are you delivering something?" But Darcy wasn't listening because right there, almost nose to nose, was a small tabby and white cat, staring curiously at her with round yellow-green eyes.

Darcy was so surprised that she half
fell over backwards. "Charlie!" she cried
loudly, and the tabby and white cat
turned tail and raced back into the flat.

"Was that Charlie?" Dad exclaimed.
"Are you OK, love? Did you hurt
yourself? I didn't see – was that him?"

Darcy only nodded. She couldn't
speak. She was quite sure it had been
Charlie, but he had taken one look at
her and run away!

"Charlie?" The old lady looked anxiously between Darcy and her dad. "I'm sorry, I don't quite… Oh!" She stared in surprise as Darcy scrambled up and raced away, pushing past Dad and out of the main door, running for home.

Charlie was in the kitchen of the flat, hunched up in a little ball under the table. His ears were flattened back and his tail was double its usual size. He was confused. He hadn't expected to see Darcy here – she belonged in his other house. He had been missing her. He'd wanted to go back, but the windows had been closed overnight and there wasn't a cat flap here, like there was at home.

He hadn't minded all that much, since the old lady had made such a fuss of him and kept giving him little treats. She'd even bought a ball that rattled when he batted it and a litter tray to go in the corner of her kitchen. But he'd kept thinking of Darcy and Will, and how good it would be to snuggle up on the end of Darcy's bed. He'd sat on the windowsill looking out at the dark garden and mewed a little, but the old lady had stroked him and tickled under his chin and he'd forgotten...

Then to see Darcy when the door opened, that hadn't been right. He didn't understand – and she had shouted! He didn't even understand why he'd run... But Darcy was gone again and now he wished he hadn't dashed away from her…

The old lady hurried into the kitchen, calling, "Puss! Come on, little one. Oh dear…"

Charlie eyed her, confused. She didn't sound right either – she wasn't shouting, but her soft voice was high and anxious now.

The old lady sat down on one of the kitchen chairs and sighed. Then she leaned over and peered at him under the table, looking between him and the piece of paper in her hand. "This is you, isn't it, puss? The little girl dropped it when she fell over. Oh, this is awful. I was so sure you were a stray when you kept coming back, and you seemed so hungry… I suppose I just wanted you not to have a home so you could stay with me."

Charlie crept closer, nudging the piece of paper with his nose.

"Yes, that's definitely a picture of you. Well, we'd better take you back. That poor girl, she was ever so upset. They're from the house over the fence, I've heard them in the garden, the girl and her little brother."

Charlie put his front paws up against the old lady's knee and tried to nibble the paper, but she scooped him up, cuddling him against her shoulder and rubbing the soft velvet of his nose. "I really must take you back. Oh dear…"

Chapter Eight

Darcy raced down the road towards home. She wasn't thinking very clearly – she was too upset to think. She just wanted to get away. That old lady had stolen Charlie! She had shut him up in her flat and made him her cat instead. "She stole him! She stole him!" Darcy whispered shakily to herself as she ran.

But the problem was, even though

she was upset, Darcy knew that wasn't really what had happened. It was only what she wanted to believe. If that old lady *had* shut Charlie up and kept him there when he hadn't wanted it, he would have raced away as soon as she opened the door. He hadn't been trying to escape when Darcy saw him – he'd just wanted to see who was at the door. It had been Darcy who'd upset him. He'd actually run away from *her*.

The old lady had adopted him. She'd probably thought he didn't have a home because he'd kept turning up in her garden and he had no collar on. They had neglected him, all of them, but especially Darcy, and Charlie had gone looking for someone to love him.

Darcy sniffed hard. He'd found

someone and he'd chosen them instead.

She shoved the front gate open
and stumbled up the path. Then she
realized that of course the front door
was locked and Dad had the keys.

Darcy sank down on the doorstep,
the last copy of their flyer in her hands.
She stared at it and a fat tear splashed
on to the photo of Charlie, blotching
his beautiful pink nose. How could
they have been so stupid and forgotten
how special he was?

"Darcy!" Dad came hurrying down the path with Mum and Will close behind him.

"What happened?" Mum demanded. "We saw you running along the road! What's wrong? Did you find him? Oh, he's not..." She stopped herself, but Darcy knew what she had been going to say – she was worried that Charlie might have been hit by a car.

Darcy sniffed. If that had happened, it would be so much worse. She felt a tiny bit more cheerful – at least Charlie was safe.

Dad reached over her to unlock the front door. "Come on, we'll explain." He pulled Darcy up gently and led her inside.

"Did you find him?" Will asked. "What happened? Why's Darcy crying? Where's Charlie?"

"At the flats," Darcy sniffed. "With an old lady. He doesn't want to be our cat any more." She pressed her hands against her eyes. "But at least he hasn't been run over, like Mum thought."

"What?" Mum put an arm round her. "Oh Darcy, were you listening to me and Dad last night?"

"I didn't mean to," Darcy muttered shakily. Then she jumped as the doorbell rang shrilly, just behind them.

Will opened the door and stood staring at the old lady on the doorstep – Charlie was clutched tightly in her arms.

She held
him out,
looking
anxious,
and Charlie
wriggled.

"I'm so
sorry. I'm Rose
Macaulay, and I
think this must be your cat."

Charlie nibbled at the little pile of
cat biscuits he'd left in his food bowl
the day before, but the old lady had
fed him that morning and he wasn't
very hungry. He padded around
the kitchen, inspecting everyone's

feet approvingly. They were all home, just where they should be. He nuzzled against Will's trainers and Will leaned down to stroke him. Charlie let Will pet him for a minute and then sprang up on to Darcy's lap, expecting to be stroked. Darcy always fussed over him.

But she only stared at him, her hand lifted uncertainly as though she wanted to stroke him but wasn't sure if she should. Charlie gazed back at her, remembering the way she'd yelled at Will the day before and then shouted at him when he peered round the door. Perhaps she didn't want him after all? He laid his ears flat and crouched a little, wondering if he should jump down.

Slowly, hesitantly, Darcy reached to rub his ears, and Charlie nudged his chin against her hand. No, it was all right. She was just the same as before. He closed his eyes and lifted his chin blissfully to the ceiling as she scratched him underneath. That was the exact place – no, there... He began to purr.

"I'm so, so sorry," Rose was explaining. "He didn't have a collar on, you see, and he looked so hungry." She sighed. "Of course, I'm sure he wasn't hungry at all. I expect he's just a very good actor. I never should have let him in that first day…"

"It's our fault," Mum said guiltily, turning round from filling the kettle for tea. "Everyone's been so busy since Darcy and Will went back to school. I should have realized that Charlie was wandering off. But I was occupied with work and we just didn't pay him enough attention."

"Well, of course I won't feed him any more. And if he comes into my garden again I'll shoo him away," Rose said, looking down at Charlie, who was curled up on Darcy's lap now, a little tabby and white bundle. Darcy saw her face twist sadly.

"You don't need to do that!" she said in a whisper, so as not to disturb the dozing kitten, and Rose looked at her in surprise. "I mean – Charlie likes you. He's allowed to have friends…" Darcy shrugged, looking embarrassed. She knew what she meant, but it sounded a bit silly.

"Darcy's right," Dad said, smiling. "If you don't mind him inviting himself in, that is."

Rose smiled rather shyly. "That's very kind of you. I still feel dreadful about accidentally stealing your cat…"

"You should be," Will said, glaring at her accusingly. "We were very worried about him!"

"Will!" Darcy gave him a shocked look. "Don't be so rude!"

But Rose shook her head, smiling. "Will reminds me very much of my grandson, Louis. He's seven."

Will looked pleased. "I'm only six, but I'm really big. Does Louis go to the same school as us? There's a Louis in Year Three, isn't there, Darcy?"

"No." Rose shook her head sadly. "He lives in London, I'm afraid, quite a long way away. But I get to chat to him on the phone every week."

Darcy looked down at Charlie and stroked the fine puffs of fur just at the bottom of his ears. She couldn't help wondering if Rose was lonely as her family didn't live close by. It felt as if she needed Charlie almost as much as they did.

"Charlie's very bad about keeping his collar on," she explained to Rose. "Do you think we could give you a spare collar, in case he comes over to you and he hasn't got one on?"

"Oh, of course!" The old lady nodded delightedly. "I'll make sure to check." She leaned over to look at Charlie on Darcy's lap. "He really is a little beauty, isn't he?" she murmured admiringly.

Darcy nodded. "The most beautiful

cat ever." She wasn't sure if Charlie heard her but he made a little *prrp* noise in his sleep and turned over on her lap, so he was lying on his back with his perfectly pink paws in the air. His tummy was all white fluff, with just a few patches of tabby spots around the edge.

"Oh, the angel," Rose said, laughing, and Darcy smiled down at Charlie, heavy and saggy and warm in her lap. Charlie was their cat – but she didn't mind sharing him, just a little.

Out Now

The Perfect
Kitten

From best-selling author
HOLLY WEBB
Illustrated by Sophy Williams

The Puppy
Who Couldn't
Sleep

From best-selling author
HOLLY WEBB
Illustrated by Sophy Williams

HOLLY WEBB

Holly Webb started out as a children's
book editor and wrote her first series for
the publisher she worked for. She has been
writing ever since, with over one hundred
books to her name. Holly lives in Berkshire,
with her husband and three children.
Holly's pet cats are always nosying around
when she is trying to type on her laptop.

For more information
about Holly Webb visit:

www.holly-webb.com

The Loneliest Kitten

Other titles by Holly Webb

The Hounds of Penhallow Hall:

Winter Stories:

Animal Stories: